# SILLY TILLY'S
## THANKSGIVING
## DINNER

An I Can Read Book®

# SILLY TILLY'S THANKSGIVING DINNER

story and pictures by
# Lillian Hoban

A TRUMPET CLUB SPECIAL EDITION

ISBN 0-590-16322-1

Copyright © 1990 by Lillian Hoban.
All rights reserved. Published by Scholastic Inc., 555 Broadway, New
York, NY 10012, by arrangement with HarperCollins Publishers.
TRUMPET and the TRUMPET logo are registered trademarks
of Scholastic Inc.

12 11 10 9 8 7 6 5 4 3 2 1          6 7 8 9/9 0 1/0

Printed in the U.S.A.

*for*
*Benjamin*

# SILLY TILLY'S
# THANKSGIVING
# DINNER

It was Thanksgiving morning.

Silly Tilly Mole

was in her garden.

The leaves were falling

all around.

"Summer is gone,"

said Tilly.

"I can't remember

where it went."

A robin flew past.

"Good-bye, Tilly,"

he called.

"It is cold, and I am

going south."

Mr. Bunny came hopping

down the path.

He had on a scarf

and mittens.

He was pulling earmuffs

down over his ears.

"I am just practicing,"
said Mr. Bunny,
"in case we get
frost tomorrow."

"Oh dear,"

said silly Tilly.

"I forgot to remember

that winter is coming.

I forgot to remember

Thanksgiving is here."

Tilly ran
down the path
to her house.

"Wait, Mr. Bunny,"

she called.

"I have something

for you."

"What did you say, Tilly?"
yelled Mr. Bunny.
"I can't hear
with these
earmuffs on."

"I said WAIT,"

called Tilly.

She turned to look

at Mr. Bunny.

17

She ran BUMP

right into a tree.

Her glasses flew off.

Mr. Bunny hopped over.

"Did you say WAIT?"

he asked.

"I did," said Tilly.

"But now my glasses are gone,

and I can't remember

why I said it."

"That's all right,"

said Mr. Bunny.

"I will sit down here

and wait for you

to remember."

Mr. Bunny sat down.

TH—WUMP!

"Uh-oh," said Mr. Bunny.

"I think I found your glasses."

"Oh, thank you," said Tilly.

"That's it!" she cried.

"I just remembered

what I forgot.

22

It is *Thanks*giving!

I am having

Thanksgiving dinner

for all of my friends.

Wait—I will get your invitation."

Tilly put on her glasses.

She ran into the house.

But her glasses were smudged,

and everything looked foggy.

"Hmm," said Tilly.

"There is fog in my house.

I can't have fog in my house
at Thanksgiving dinner."
Tilly opened the window
to shoo the fog out.
But the fog
would not
go away.

"Tilly," called Mr. Bunny.

"I am still waiting

for my invitation."

"Oh dear," said Tilly.

"I forgot to remember

where I put the invitations,

and it is so foggy,

I cannot see

where they are.

I will get a broom

and sweep the fog out."

Tilly ran to the kitchen

to get a broom.

But she could not see.

She bumped

into the stove.

"Just in time to cook
Thanksgiving dinner,"
said Tilly.
She ran to the cupboard
to get pots and pans.

But she forgot

where she was going.

She went to the table

and got some cards instead.

"Here are the invitations,"

she said.

"Mr. Bunny," she called.

"Here is your invitation."

Mr. Bunny hopped up

to the door.

"Are they all for me?"

he asked.

"Oh dear," said Tilly.

"I forgot.

There is one for Mrs. Squirrel,

and one for Mr. Woodchuck,

and one for Mr. Chipmunk,

and some more besides.

But I forgot to remember

to send them."

"That's all right,"

said Mr. Bunny.

"I will give them out

on my way home."

Mr. Bunny looked at the cards.

The first card said,

MRS. SQUIRREL'S ACORN JAM
MASH A BOWL OF ACORNS
ADD A CUP OF SUGAR
STIR AND COOK OVER LOW HEAT

The next card was

the recipe for

*MR. WOODCHUCK'S*

*PINE NUT CAKE*

The next card was

the recipe for

*MR. CHIPMUNK'S*

*CRANBERRY STEW*

The next card was

the recipe for

*MRS. FIELDMOUSE'S*

*OAT BRAN*

*PUDDING*

The last card was

the recipe for

*MR. BUNNY'S*

*SWEET POTATO PIE*

"Yum, yum," said Mr. Bunny.

"What a great idea.

This is going to be

the best Thanksgiving dinner!"

Mr. Bunny hopped off

to give out the cards.

Tilly hurried into the kitchen

to start cooking.

"Now where are

all those recipes?"

she asked.

She hurried over to her desk.

But she could not see,

and she forgot

what she was

looking for.

"Oh dear," she said.
"It is getting late
and I am tired.
I will sit near the fire
and try to remember
what I forgot."

Tilly sat down

near the fire.

She fell asleep.

When she woke up,

it was dark.

"Almost time

for Thanksgiving dinner,"

she said.

"Almost time

for my guests to arrive."

Tilly got up

to set the table.

"Oh dear!" she cried.
"I just remembered
what I forgot!
It is so foggy,
I could not see
to find the recipes.
I never cooked
Thanksgiving dinner!"

Tilly started
to sniffle.
Her eyes filled
with tears.

Just then

the door flew open.

"Who is there?"

called Tilly.

She wiped her eyes.

Then she wiped her glasses.

The fog was gone

and she could see!

She saw Mrs. Squirrel
carrying a bowl
of acorn jam.
She saw Mr. Woodchuck
with a pine nut cake.
She saw Mr. Chipmunk
with a pot
of cranberry stew.
She saw Mrs. Fieldmouse
with some oat bran pudding.
And she saw Mr. Bunny
carrying a sweet potato pie!

"Oh, how lovely!"
cried Tilly.
"Now we can have
Thanksgiving dinner!"

But just as they
sat down to eat,
they heard:

GOBBLE! GOBBLE!

GOBBLE!

The front door flew open.

In came Mr. Turkey

with a bag of corn.

"Tilly Mole,"
said Mr. Turkey,
"don't you know
you can't have Thanksgiving
without Mr. Turkey?"

"Oh, Mr. Turkey,"
said Tilly,
"*everybody* knows that!
I just forgot to remember
to give Mr. Bunny
your invitation."

So they all had
Thanksgiving dinner.

Then they sat

around the fire

and sang songs.

Mr. Turkey

made his recipe for

*MR. TURKEY'S*

*BEST EVER*

*POPCORN.*

And everybody said it was
the best Thanksgiving ever.